MOUSE AND MOLE

Joyce Dunbar

Illustrated by

James Mayhew

PICTURE CORGI BOOKS

MOUSE AND MOLE
A PICTURE CORGI BOOK : 0 552 52704 1

First published in Great Britain by Doubleday,
a division of Transworld Publishers Ltd

PRINTING HISTORY
Doubleday edition published 1993
Picture Corgi edition published 1994
Reprinted 1994

Picture Corgi Books are published by Transworld Publishers Ltd,
61–63 Uxbridge Road, Ealing, London W5 5SA,
in Australia by Transworld Publishers (Australia) Pty Ltd,
15–25 Helles Avenue, Moorebank, NSW 2170,
and New Zealand by Transworld Publishers (NZ) Ltd,
3 William Pickering Drive, Albany, Auckland.

Made and printed in Portugal
by Printer Portuguesa

~ For dear old Frog and Toad ~

CONTENTS

Talk to Me

'Talk to me,' said Mouse.

'What about?' said Mole.

'Anything,' said Mouse.

'I can't think of anything,' said Mole. 'Give me some ideas.'

'You could tell me what we are going to do tomorrow,' said Mouse.

'What are we going to do tomorrow?' said Mole.

'Well,' said Mouse. 'If it is a fine day we are going on a picnic in the woods. We are making cheese and cucumber sandwiches and we are taking our new picnic basket with cups and saucers and plates.'

'So we are,' said Mole. 'But what if it isn't a fine day?'

'If it isn't a fine day,' said Mouse, 'we are going to make an apple wood fire. We will sit in our cosy armchairs and roast chestnuts and toast muffins. We will have hot chocolate to drink.'

'So we will,' said Mole. 'But what if it's an in-between sort of day?'

'We will do something in-between,' said Mouse. 'We will tidy up.'

'So we will,' said Mole.

'Thank you for talking to me,' said Mouse.

'That's all right,' said Mole.

Salad

Mole's snout peeped out of the bedclothes.

'What sort of day is it?' he asked.

'Wild and wintry,' said Mouse.

Mole snuggled his snout back down. 'In that case I'll stay in bed.'

'Don't you worry,' said Mouse. 'I will make an apple wood fire in the sitting room. Then you will want to get up.'

Mouse made an apple wood fire. Mole's snout sniffed
apple wood smoke. Soon he was shuffling downstairs.
'How I hate these wild and wintry days,' he grumbled.
'All we can do is huddle by the fire.'
'We can do more than that,' said Mouse. 'We can toast
some muffins. We can roast some chestnuts.'
'Good,' said Mole. 'I'm hungry.'
So Mouse toasted some muffins and roasted some chestnuts.

'Are there any more?' asked Mole when he had eaten a plateful.

'Are there any more?' Mole asked again when he had eaten a second plateful.

'I've eaten too much,' said Mole when he had eaten a third plateful. 'Tomorrow I will eat only salad.'
'That's a good idea,' said Mouse.
'It is,' said Mole. 'So why wait? I will start my diet now. Have we got any salad, Mouse?'
'We have,' said Mouse. 'We have carrots and radishes and spinach.'
'Then I'll have some,' said Mole, and he ate a plateful of salad.

'Aren't I good?' he said. 'I have eaten all that salad. I think I deserve a little treat. Butter some muffins, Mouse. Roast a few more of those chestnuts.'

Then Mole ate another plateful. 'Wintry days are not so bad after all,' he said, falling into a snooze.

Tidying up

'Hurray!' said Mouse the next morning. 'The sun is shining today. Today we can go on our picnic!'

'No we can't,' said Mole. 'I ate too much yesterday. I ate toasted muffins and salad. Then I ate more toasted muffins. Today I will eat nothing at all. I will do exercises instead.'

But when Mole went into the sitting room to do his exercises, he found it was all of a clutter.

'We will have to tidy up, Mouse. I need some space to bend and stretch.'

So Mouse bent down and picked all the clutter up from the floor. Mole collected all the bits and bobs from the shelves. Mouse cleared away all the odds and ends from the sofa. They piled everything into the kitchen.

'There!' said Mouse when they had finished. 'Now there's room for you to bend and stretch!'
'But what about my deep breathing?' said Mole. 'I need fresh air for deep breathing. Here there is too much dust. We will have to dust and sweep, Mouse.'

So Mouse got down on his four paws and swept the floor. Mole stretched on tiptoe to dust the cobwebs off the ceiling and shelves. They worked so hard that soon they were out of breath.

'Phew!' panted Mouse when they had finished. 'I'm puffed. But now you can do your exercises.'
'Exercises!' said Mole. 'I'm too exhausted to exercise! What I need is a cup of tea. Come on, Mouse. Follow me into the kitchen. We deserve a cup of tea.'

But when they went into the kitchen to make a cup of tea,
they found it was all of a clutter.

'Mouse,' said Mole. 'We will have to tidy up. There's no room to make a cup of tea.'

So together they tidied up the kitchen. They scooped up all the bits and bobs. They gathered in all the odds and ends. Then they bundled them into the bedroom. It took them the rest of the day.

'There!' said Mole when they had finished. 'We've tidied up the sitting room. We've tidied up the kitchen. We deserve a cup of tea and something to eat as well. How about pancakes and treacle?'

So Mouse made a pile of pancakes while Mole got out a tin of treacle.

'I need an early night after that,' said Mole when he had finished.

'So do I,' said Mouse.

But when they went into the bedroom for their early night, they found it was all of a clutter.

'Mouse,' said Mole. 'Just look at my bed. It is covered with odds and ends.'

'And just look at mine,' said Mouse. 'It is piled with bits and bobs.'

They flopped into bed just the same. They were much too
tired to care...

Stuff

'Help!' cried Mole the next morning. 'I am being buried alive.'

'I know just how you feel,' said Mouse. 'Come on. We will have to tidy up.'

'But we tidied up yesterday,' said Mole.

'We did. But we did it all wrong,' said Mouse. 'The problem, you see, is stuff. We've got too much stuff. We didn't tidy it up at all. We moved it from room to room. We need to get rid of it altogether.'

'But I like stuff,' said Mole. 'Stuff is very interesting. It might come in useful one day.'

'You can have stuff, or you can have space,' said Mouse.
'But you can't have both.'
'But what is the use of space if you have no stuff to put in
it?' asked Mole.
'Space is space,' said Mouse, 'and stuff is stuff. Come on.
Let's take some stuff to the rubbish dump and we can have
some space for a change. Help me to fill these sacks.'

Together they filled three sacks.
'You are right, Mouse,' said Mole when they had finished.
'Look at all this lovely space. No more tidying up! No
more stuff to tidy!'

'We can take these sacks on the motorbike,' said Mouse.
'Whose turn is it to drive?'
'Mine,' said Mole. 'Same as last time.'
There were three big skips at the rubbish dump. One was
marked 'Glass'. Another was marked 'Paper'. A third was
marked 'Metal'.
Mouse threw all the newspapers into the skip marked
'Paper'. 'That's that!' he said.

'But look at that bundle of comics,' said Mole. 'They look
very interesting. I must take them home.'
And he filled up the sack with old comics.

Then Mouse threw all the empty jars and bottles into the
skip marked 'Glass'. 'That's that!' he said.
'But look at that old mirror,' said Mole, 'and that fish tank.
I must take them home. You never know, they might
come in useful.'
And he put them into a sack.
Mouse threw all the old tin cans and old pans into the skip
marked 'Metal'. 'That's that!' he said.
'But look at those coathangers, and that old tin trunk, and
those metal springs. I must take them home. They might
come in useful,' said Mole.
And he filled up the last of the sacks.

So Mole and Mouse rode home, carrying three sacks full of
stuff.
'How clever you are to think of making all that space,' said
Mole. 'Now we have somewhere to put all this stuff.'

He tipped the comics on to the sofa in the sitting room.
He put the fish tank and the mirror on the shelves. He
emptied the coathangers and the tin trunk and the metal
springs on to the floor. There was no room left for Mouse
and Mole.

Mouse scratched his head.

'As I was saying, Mole, you can have stuff, or you can have
space, but you can't have both. We will have to stay
outside.'

Mouse sat down on the steps. Mole twiddled a broken
spring. 'I brought this one especially for you,' said Mole.
But Mouse wasn't pleased. Not a bit!

The Picnic

'I think we should go on our picnic today,' said Mouse.
'I feel like a good long walk.'
'So do I,' said Mole. 'But what about the weather?'
'It's fine,' said Mouse. 'The sun is shining and there's hardly a cloud in the sky.'
'In that case I shall wear my T-shirt and shorts and sun hat,' said Mole.
'And I will pack the hamper,' said Mouse.

Soon they were ready to go. They had just reached the gate when Mole suddenly stopped stock still.

'I can see a cloud!' he said.

'It's only a little cloud,' said Mouse. 'It will soon go away.'

'It might get bigger,' said Mole. 'It might be a rain cloud. I must put on my mackintosh and galoshes and sou'wester.' While Mouse was waiting for Mole, he couldn't resist a little dip into the hamper. He ate three of the cheese and cucumber sandwiches.

'Here I am!' said Mole at last. 'Ready to face the rain!'
They had walked along a little way when Mole stopped in
his tracks.
'That cloud is definitely getting bigger,' he said to Mouse,
'and I can feel a chill wind getting up. You never know,
Mouse, it might snow. I must go back for my woolly hat
and scarf and mittens.'
While Mouse waited for Mole, he couldn't resist a little dip
into the hamper. He had some biscuits and some lime
juice cordial.

'Here I am!' said Mole at last. 'Ready to face any weather!
I have my woolly things on top, and my rain things
underneath, and my sun things underneath that.'

They had walked a little way further when Mole stopped
still once more.
'What about my pyjamas?' he said.
'What about your pyjamas?' asked Mouse.
'We might walk so far on our picnic that we might not get
back in time for bed,' said Mole. 'I must go back for my
pyjamas just in case.'

While Mouse waited for Mole, he couldn't resist a little dip into the hamper. He ate some crisps, some iced buns and two apples.

'Here I am!' said Mole at last. 'I have got my pyjamas. And guess what? I have remembered my swimming things as well. You never know, we might find a place to swim.'

'But you don't like swimming,' said Mouse.

'So I don't,' said Mole. 'I forgot.'

Mouse brushed some crumbs from his whiskers. 'Mole,' he said. 'Have you had a good long walk?'

'Why, yes I have, come to think of it,' said Mole. 'With all that to-ing and fro-ing.'

'Good,' said Mouse, 'because we are not going on a picnic after all.'

'Why not?' said Mole.

'Because I have eaten all the food in the hamper,' said Mouse.

'I thought there might be an emergency,' said Mole, 'so guess what?'

'What?' said Mouse.

'I have packed another picnic in my pockets. Why don't we sit down right here and eat it?'

'You can eat it, Mole. I'm full up. I'm going for a good long walk.'

And Mouse did.